LA FAMILLE BILINGUE

AND

A SIMPLY MISSING

By Gregory John Ferris

La Famille Bilingue

A play in two acts

By

Gregory John Ferris

À Madame Linda Fenouil

La Famille Bilingue a été représentée pour la première fois
à Louisville, Kentucky le 15 juillet 2017, dans une mise en scène
de Cristina Martin, décors et costumes de James Ballard

CHARACTERS

Guillaume   (Julien Fenouil)

> French, husband of Simone. Teacher of chemistry in French high school in Montpellier, France. Has an interest in perfume manufacturing.

Simone   (Sarah Isaacs)

> French, part-time instructor in English in a French elementary school, and enthused about American culture.

Mark   (Tracey Dunn)

> American, husband of Audrey, resident of Louisville, Kentucky, employed with a large, local adult beverages company.

Audrey   (Jessica Vautard)

> American, professor of French at a Louisville university, Francophile

Georges   (Liam Scott)

> French, 19, son of Guillaume and
> Simone. Foreign exchange student
> for the upcoming summer, about
> which he is not excited.

Avril/April   (Shannon Frazier)

> American, 19, daughter of Mark and
> Audrey, who will be an exchange
> student in France during Georges'
> upcoming summer stay.

Melanie Buddie   (Megan Randell)

> American, middle-aged, talkative
> and bubbly, she is the sole
> proprietor of a small catering
> business.

SETTING

Act I, a Manhattan hotel, mid July, 1977

Act II, a residence in Louisville, KY, May 2,3, 1997

TIME

Act I, scene 1, late evening

Act I, scene 2, the next morning

Act II, scene 1, mid morning

Act II, scene 2, 1 hour later

Act II, scene 3, the same day, early evening

Act II, scene 4, later that same night

ACT I

SCENE 1

(Salon of a suite in a Manhattan Hotel, bedrooms at stages left and right. Guillaume , Simone, Mark and Audrey enter. All in mid to late 20s, and all a bit tipsy. Window, overlooking the street is the audience)

MARK: J'aime bien New York. Le bruit, La foule, c'est comme une réunion familiale, entouré d'enfants peu connus. Ces gosses-là sont de bonnes sentinelles, tant aussi long qu'ils crient, tout va bien.

SIMONE: Comme les oiseaux dans une forêt.

MARK :   C'est exact. En revanche, le silence d'une forêt, ou d'une ville, ca signale « danger ».

SIMONE: You're funny. After 90 minutes of Sartre you have become a veritable philosopher. It is good for us that we saw his play HUIS CLOS,

No Exit, tonight, and not the Jack the Ripper musical that the concierge suggested.

AUDREY: Quant à moi, 90 minutes de Sartre, c'est largement assez. La difficulté commence même avec son nom. D'autre coté, celui du philosophe Pascal est plus facile en anglais. « Pascal » sonne comme une boisson sucrée, comme Pepsi. Avaler une gorgée de Pascal, il est on ne peut plus facile. Alors que Sartre, Sarte, en entendant Sarte, je me dis au secours, au secours.

SIMONE: Et voilà, Il y est. The anti-philosopher and the philosopher, married one to another. To me, it is like the fashion world ; Pascal is démodé, out of style. Everyone understands him but no one agrees with his ideas any longer. With Sartre *(pronounces the name slowly to Audrey)* ,it is just the opposite. Everyone agrees with him, it is just that no one understands him.

MARK: *(laughing)*, Désormais, je dois renommer Audrey, Sartre. I agree with her but…

AUDREY: *(playful slap to Mark's arm)*. Parlons d'autres choses. Ca fait cinq ans depuis mon séjour

à Montpellier. Regarder toi, Guillaume, m'y
ramene.

SIMONE: Yes, five years ago. You were in
Montpellier for a month Audrey, and myself, I spent
that same July in Louisville. My four weeks there,
with the cities' exchange program was the
beginning for me.

AUDREY: De quoi?

SIMONE: D'une immersion dans la vie
américaine. Pas la vie réele, tu sais. Tout
ressemblait plutôt à une scène de théâtre. C'est un
rêve à moitié oublié. A partir de ce moment-là, je
ne me suis décidé à jurer par les choses américaines.

MARK: *(smiling)* Tu es devenue une vrai
américaine, sans connaitre ni la langue, ni la
culture, ni l'histoire du pays. Je t'ai trouvée si
mignonne.

GUILLAUME :   To become American without
knowing the language, the culture, the history.
From what I have seen today, that describes the half
of New York.

MARK: But New York is a city of immigrants, Guillaume . They are half of the city's population.

GUILLAUME :   You're correct, bien sûr. But I was speaking of the other half, the natives, the native non-speakers. You find that they are speaking English, these true New Yorkers ?

MARK: Touché.

AUDREY: While you were Americanizing, Simone, I was surrendering myself to all things French in Montpellier.

GUILLAUME : (to Audrey): All things? Tu as essayé tout? You missed one or two of us, of them. I am sure of it.

AUDREY: Such as?

SIMONE: Sans doute, veut-il dire, les escargots, le boudin noir…. le boudin blanc.

AUDREY: (perplexed) Le boudin blanc, Celui-la avait dû m'échapper, quand même il me reste du temps.

(All but Simone sit)

SIMONE: Du vin? (passes glasses around)

ALL: Yes !

(Simone searches for a corkscrew without success).

SIMONE: Oh yes, the American hotel. Aucun tire-bouchon.

MARK: No corkscrew?

SIMONE: Non, qu'est ce qu'on va faire?

MARK: (removes Swiss army knife from pocket) J'étais scout il y des années. Voilà, American ingenuity.

GUILLAUME : (passes opened knife to Simone, while pausing to look at it) Ah, yes, American ingenuity, made in Switzerland.

MARK: I meant having it with me.

(Simone takes some time to open the wine, during which :)

AUDREY: (looking around) This is an odd room, why is there a photograph of Muhammad Ali on the wall? He is from Louisville, you know. What a strange coincidence that we are from there as well and have booked this room.

MARK: I'm not sure. We needed a suite with a second bedroom. This room was available.

SIMONE: Muhammed Ali y a passee la nuit après le match qu'il a perdu contre Joe Frazier (pronounces it FRAH Z YAY) en 1974.

MARK : Oh, yes. The first Ali-Frazier fight. You're correct Simone, Frazier won. I think.

GUILLAUME :   Depuis quand tu t'y connais en boxe?

SIMONE: Not very long, I read the description underneath the photo.

(Pours wine for all)

GUILLAUME: Mark, Louisville -- Kentucky is well known for its good bourbon, but not for wine, oui? Simone tells me that you are with a distillery?

MARK: Yes, one of the largest. But we are looking to expand, probably into the wine business; some of the vintages that I've sampled recently in California have been very good.

AUDREY: C'est drôle. Dans l'Amérique d'autrefois, on y trouvait du bon bourbon mais du mauvais vin, alors qu'en France on trouvait du bon vin mais de mauvais Bourbons.

(All but Mark laugh at the pun)

AUDREY: It was a pun, un jeu de mot. Bourbon versus Bourbons. Les anciens rois français.

MARK: Ah, j'y suis. In Kentucky, one does not joke about bourbon.

GUILLAUME :   En France, non plus.

MARK: Guillaume, votre, pardon, ton métier, si je comprends bien, est parfumier, tu es proprietaire d'une parfumerie?

SIMONE: A mi-temps. Only part time, the perfume business is more a hobby.

GUILLAUME: Simone, ce que tu viens de dire, c'était le cas, non plus. C'est un métier.

SIMONE: Qu'est ce-que tu dis? Je t'ai deja dit - Je ne suis pas d'accord avec ta décision.

GUILLAUME (takes a sip of wine and looking at Mark, continues) : Oui, c'est exact, depuis ma jeunesse, je travaille en tant que parfumier, juste à côté de mon père, de la même façon qu'il l'avait fait à côté du sien. Il y a quelques années, il en a eu marre, et l'entreprise est tombée entre mes mains.

SIMONE: Quelle entreprise. Mark, Audrey, you must understand that this business is little more than a hobby, even worse, it is a family obsession. At least Guillaume went to university for his diplôme in chemistry. As long as he can teach at the school, this, this bricolage

AUDREY: Tinkering?

SIMONE: Tinkering? Yes, this tinkering is harmless.

GUILLAUME: Arrête de raconter mon histoire. Simone, tu aime toi aussi bricoler. (Gives her a quick peck on the cheek)

A vrai dire, ce que dit Simone parait vraisemblable. J'admets que, vu de l'extérieur, les hommes de ma famille souffrent tous de cette maladie, de cette foi.

AUDREY :   Quelle foi ?

GUILLAUME :   La foi en nous-même.

Mon pere et mon grand pere se croyaient etre le
prochain phenomene du monde des parfums. On a
cherché à créer un mélange entre les fleurs d'Europe
et celles d'Amérique du sud. On avait comme
modèle, comme but à atteindre, le grand succès de
Shalimar, un mélange d'est et d'ouest.

SIMONE: And both of them failed, so often that
the neighbors said that they were crazy fools.

AUDREY: That is sad. And yet you persevere,
Guillaume?

GUILLAUME: Ce n'est pas aussi grave que
Simone le peint. They weren't crazy, insane. It
became more a family joke, almost English, in that
it was bizarre (pause) eccentric. Yes, eccentric like
an Anglais. My father would celebrate each new
discovery with too much wine, and the next
morning would have forgotten the formula and
would need to start his work over again.

MARK :   He never wrote it down ?

GUILLAUME :   Il avait peur de l'espionnage.

SIMONE: On dit, on recommence par le recommencement.

(Mark laughs by himself)

SIMONE :   En bref, toute l'histoire. Too much wine, too many spies, two lives wasted.

(Awkward moment)

SIMONE: Guillame n'en est pas moins prof de chimie. Cela nous suffit. In 24 hours, he will have dropped this silly dream, this mirage will have evaporated.

MARK: What do you mean, in 24 hours?

AUDREY: (takes another sip), This sounds very mysterious. (Nestles close to Guillaume and away from Mark)   24 hours? A race against time, Guillaume ? Une veritable course contre le montre ?

MARK :   No spies, I hope.

SIMONE: This is why we have come to New York.

AUDREY. Guillaume, you've come to New York on business? Not to see me, to see us?

Quel mystere. Raconte.

GUILLAUME :   Wait here, i will return in a minute. (exits stage left).

SIMONE :   After the meeting tomorrow with this American « Beauty products company » (sarcastic), life should return to normal. I say return to normal, as if we resided there once. Life should be, will be, normal. I can tolerate another day of obsession.

GUILLAUME (enters stage left. He takes a small red velvet bag from his jacket pocket and removes from it a vial full of a light blue liquid) : Voilà ma pièce de résistance, mon chef d'œuvre.

SIMONE: Tu en a eu d'autre?

GUILLAUME: D'autre quoi?

SIMONE: D'autre pièces , d'autre œuvres.

GUILLAUME: (embarrassed) Pour être précis, ceci est ma première.

(Guillaume raises vial and looks around at others while they regard the vial, then turn their eyes to him)

GUILLAUME: Assis parmi des amis, among friends, the events of today are an omen. To see a play of Sartre the very day before my meeting with an American perfume company is more than a coincidence.

MARK: Not a French company? That seems unusual.

SIMONE: The French companies are very familiar with this family's obsession. They declined all of the requests to meet with Guillaume. I only came along to New York in order to see old friends (winks at Mark), and to shop.

MARK: I see. Hmmm.

GUILLAUME: Parlons de moi. (regards vial). Sartre a écrit un grand œuvre, l'être et le néant, un chef d'œuvre et à la fois, un livre incompréhensible. Regardez, je vous présente "Le Neant". My perfume, Oblivion.

SIMONE: Il en a déjà écrit la première publicité.

(All laugh easily)

GUILLAUME: I wanted to share this unveiling of the new world/ old world perfume, with a good friend (corrects himself) with friends here in the new world.

(Guillaume opens vial and passes it around for all to smell)

AUDREY: Ca sent merveilleusement bon.

SIMONE: Ce n'est que du parfum. Penses-tu que celui-ci a mérité un tel voyage ici à New York? (She applies some) C'est du parfum. Et après?

AUDREY: Wait! Simone, you have not tried this perfume before ?   Not in France ?

SIMONE: Of course not. Il a fallu le dévoiler ici, auprès de toi, apparemment. (Simone appears a little dazed)

MARK: DAY VWAL A?

SIMONE: Dévoiler. To unveil. (Simone extends her arm under the nose of Mark and says seductively) Dévoile-moi. (catches herself). That would mean, Unveil me, for example

MARK: Ahh, Ca sent bon. (blinks several times).

Je me rappelle une poème:

SIMONE: Celui de Verlaine?

MARK: Verlaine? Je ne sais pas. Ecoute

L'absence est à l'amour ce qu'est au feu le vent, il éteint le petit, il allume le grand.

SIMONE: C'est belle Mark.

MARK: (shakes head): Eh, Guillaume, what gives the perfume its blue tint?

GUILLAUME: Le teint bleu? Toujours tout de droit au point chez les Américains. Tu te connais en fleurs?

MARK: Flowers? Not very much. I thought that perfume is sourced from animals.

(Audrey applies some perfume, and returns vial to Simone)

GUILLAUME: C'est exacte, mais de nos jours, je crois que tout est sur le point de changer. Moi, je préfère n'utilise que des ingrédients botanique, d'autant plus que nous habitons le sud. D'ailleurs je dois à mon père cet effort.

MARK: Alors, le bleu?

(Audrey extends her arm under the nose of Guillaume)

AUDREY: (to Guillaume): Dévoile-moi. (Winks at Simone).

GUILLAUME (drily) C'est tout à fait ce que j'attendais. L'odeur se repand presque immediatement. Il n'y a pas besoin d'attendre dix minutes pour que le parfum fasse son effet.

AUDREY and SIMONE: The perfume achieves its
effect. (they giggle)

GUILLAUME: The blue tint, you question. The
blue comes from a rare orchid in central and south
America, which the experts call the Blue Vanda. I
was able to bring several back to France before it
was declared under danger, to be endangered. The
blue vanda provides this color, no dyes are used, but
it is more integral than just the color.

A mes yeux c'est de la magie. Cette orchidée est au
parfum, ce qu'est au pain le leveur. The blue vanda
is like yeast to the bread.

MARK: J'ai soif (extends wine glass to Simone).

(Simone deliberately misunderstands and sniffs his
forearm and then, sets her glass down to fill his.
She needs do to this as she is still holding the open
vial. Simone then puts the vial in the same hand
holding the bottle, over the opening, and picks up
her own glass, and sighs) Ca sent bon. (Not clear if
she means Mark or the wine). (giggles, then drops
vial into the bottle, seen clearly by audience but not
by the cast.

Lights go out on stage.

ALL or SOME: Qu'est-ce qui se passe? What happened? (Fumbling sounds, 30 seconds go by)

SIMONE: (lights and holds a lit match)

MARK: Pass me the matches, I will try the light switch. (Walks to wall with lit match, switch doesn't work. Tries another, no effect. Returns to group)

SIMONE: J'ai une bougie (and lights a small candle) (Simone stands and walks toward window overlooking the street, front of stage, looks out for a minute) Je me sens très mal (runs to MARK). Suis-je aveugle? New York a disparu.

MARK: It must be another blackout, une coupuer de courante.

AUDREY: Well, we still have wine (and pour some for the men).

GUILLAUME: Je trouve que ce vin est meilleur bu dans le noir.

MARK: Tu as raison. Tant mieux.

All sit quietly and drink for a minute.

MARK : Guillaume, what time is your appointment tomorrow ?

GUILLAUME : Appointment ?

MARK : Ton rendez-vous ?

GUILLAUME : Rendez-vous ? Avec qui ?

AUDREY : The one with Pascal or Pepsi ? Its about a play, you were saying.

SIMONE : I dont want to see a play tomorrow, we are here on vacation and I am going shopping.

MARK: I'm a bit woozy (staggers to feet and heads to a bedroom).

GUILLAUME: Moi aussi. Je vais me coucher. Quelle journée. (Rises and shuffles to other bedroom door).

MARK: Coming honey?

GUILLAUME: Chérie?

(Candle goes out).

END ACT I SCENE 1

Act I Scene 2

The next morning.

Bedroom door opens and out steps Simone (from stage right. She walks to front of stages and peers out the window.

SIMONE: New York, la ville qui ne dort jamais. Arrête de hurler. (Groans and shuffles to shared bathroom, sound of running water)

AUDREY (exits a minute later from other bedroom, from stage left, walks to bathroom and hears running water, shrugs and goes to collapse on couch. Wine glasses and a nearly empty bottle are on the floor).

(A minute passes).

GUILLAUME (exits from same bedroom as had Audrey, and shuffles to bathroom, mumbles): Bonjour Audrey.

AUDREY (jumps, after a double take and eyes wide open): Bonjour. Simone is in there.

GUILLAUME: Simone, Dépêche-toi, s'il te plait. (Shuffles back to bedroom and closes the door)

(After a minute Simone exits and heads to stage right bedroom)

(Audrey enters bathroom)

SIMONE: C'est à toi, cheri (just as stage right door opens and Mark enters).

MARK: What's mine?

SIMONE: What?

MARK: Yes.

SIMONE: Yes, what?

MARK: Never mind. Is Guillaume awake? Was he sleeping when you awoke?

SIMONE: What?

MARK: (chuckling) You seem to have forgotten English in one day, Simone. Guillame, s-est-il réveille?

SIMONE: Non, no, I mean yes, I think so.

MARK: That clear. Lets stay with what until after breakfast.

SIMONE: What?

MARK: Perfect. (walks over to stage left bedroom, Simone is looking back and forth, confused. Mark raps on door). Guillaume, are you alive in there? (waits a few seconds and raps again)

GUILLAUME: Attends, j'ai la gueule de bois.

(Mark turns back to center stage, and Audrey exits from bathroom).

AUDREY (relieved to see Mark apparently coming from the 'correct', stage left bedroom):   Mark honey, can you go back in the room and fetch me my bra?

MARK (walking toward stage right bedroom): Sure.

AUDREY (panicky):   Oh never mind, I have it.

MARK: (incredulous) You have it?

AUDREY: What?

MARK: You just asked me….

AUDREY: What?

MARK: Never mind. Breakfast is really needed for you two, I see. How much did I have to drink last night?

SIMONE: I only see the one bottle, and it is not even empty.

(Mark enters stage right bedroom)

GUILLAUME (exits with bra in hand) C'est à qui (and begins walking towards Simone)

AUDREY (tries to stifles herself): Me.

(Guillaume passes bra to Simone, who stands, walks to bathroom, pushes Audrey into it and closes the door behind them).

MARK (enters stage right): Oh there you are. I feel as bad as you look. What did we drink last night? I remember coming to New York, and waking up this morning, but everything in between is fuzzy.

GUILLAUME: Quel jour sommes-nous?

MARK: (looks at watch) Today is Thursday, the 14th, according to my watch. Bastille Day.

GUILLAUME: What?

MARK: The 14th of July, Bastille Day.

GUILLAUME: What?

MARK: Breakfast for three, apparently.

GUILLAUME (walks toward bottle, says over shoulder): Ah, Bastille Day in Amérique, le quatorze juillet. (picks up bottle, looks at label). De la Californie, cela explique tout.

(looks more closely at bottles and shakes it, rattle heard, pours it into glass, picks up vial):   Qu'est-ce que c'est que ça? Drôle d'idée. (passes it to Mark who has approached)

MARK: It must be a marketing idea, like the worm in tequila, or the gold flakes in goldwasser. (passes it back to Guillaume, who drops it and the bottle in a waste paper basket). I wish that the girls would hurry, I'm still not feeling well.

GUILLAUME: Tu connais bien les femmes. Elles aiment causer, surtout à huis clos.

(Audrey and Simone enter stage from bathroom)

MARK: Huit clos? Isn't that a play by Sartre? I think that it is showing here in New York. Would you like to see it? Audrey, Simone, are you up to seeing a play by Sartre this afternoon or evening?

SIMONE: Absolument! Mais après que les grands magasins seront fermées. J'en parlais à Guillaume avant de partir de la France. (notices photograph of Muhammed Ali on wall) Pourquoi a-t-on monté une photographie d'un boxeur dans cette chambre? C'est tellement bizarre.

GUILLAUME: Rien qu'un objet d'art américain.

AUDREY: Simone, do you and Guillaume have plans for today?

SIMONE: Je ne sais pas. Je n'en suis pas sûr. Chéri?

GUILLAUME: Rien de tout. Audrey, nous sommes libres toute la journée.

MARK: Perfect, we have the whole day free then. Continuons.

End ACT 1

ACT 2

SCENE 1

(The living room of a home in Louisville, Kentucky, on Friday, May 2, 1997 (Oaks Day), one day before the

running of the
Kentucky
Derby)

(Doorbell rings, Audrey enters, crosses stage to
answer it)

MELANIE (standing in the doorway, holding cake):
Hi Audrey, I'm right on time, you did say 10
o'clock? Or should I say "Dix heures"? (laughs)

AUDREY: Yes, -- oui, dix heures. Thanks so
much for being punctual, its been a hectic morning.
Come on in.

MELANIE (a few steps onto stage): A qui vous le
dites?

AUDREY (pleasantly surprised) : Very good
Melanie, really impressive. You've only been
studying French with me for a few weeks. Its clear
that you are devoting effort to it.

MEL: Just call me Mel, Audrey, everyone does, except my husband Ed and my girls, who calls me Queen Mel. Anyway, I have free time while the cakes are baking. I practice my French with them.

AUDREY: Your girls ?

MEL : No, they're both out of the house. I'm not as young as I look.

AUDREY: Then who?

MEL: No, not who, what.

AUDREY: What?

MEL: The cakes.

AUDREY: What? You speak French to the cakes?

MEL: Yes, they seem to like it. At least they haven't told me to talk to Ed.

AUDREY: I think that I understand now. You tried speaking French with Ed and he told you to speak to your cakes?

MEL: He was really enthused about this French thing until he realized I meant speaking it. I don't know why he was confused. So, where would you like this?

AUDREY (pointing to table in front of various family/friend photos): Just there, please.

MEL (places cake on leaning platform so that it is somewhat visible to audience, on cake in large print: BIENVENUE A LOUISVILLE and signed Audrey, Mark and Avpril)

(On the back of Mel's shirt, slogan, BUSY BUDDIE, WHEN YOU'RE TOO BUSY, CALL A BUDDIE.   MEL BUDDIE CATERING)

(Mel regards photos):   So these are your French friends? The ones that are arriving today?

AUDREY (quick glance while doing some other work). Yes, they should be here soon.

Mark is fetching them from the airport.

MEL: Well, your son certainly takes after your husband.

AUDREY (startled): What do you mean?

MEL (slowly) Votre fils and votre mari. Ils... Ils,,,, Your son ressembles his father a great deal

AUDREY (laughs nervously). Oh, the boy, I should say young man now, is not our son, that's Georges. His parents are Guillaume and Simone. The girl, correction, young lady, is ours. She is named AVRIL. (she approaches photo of Georges) I don't see any resemblance at at. Pas du tout. Not at all.

MEL: PAH DO TOO (bad pronunciation, takes out pen and writes it down) (another glance at the photo) Let me bring in the rest of the food and the flowers from the car. (Makes one or more trips, placing flowers and various boxes on the table). Audrey, you said that your daughter is Avril?

AUDREY: Yes.

MEL: Then who is AVPRIL (spells, pointing to cake) ?   That is what you asked me to write on the cake.

AUDREY: That's a family joke.

MEL: Oh that is a relief. At first I thought it must be the name of a dog, one sees everything in this business. If you lived in Oldham county, I would have said the name of a horse, especially at this time of year. So is that the French spelling of April?

AUDREY: I call it franglais, neither French nor English, and yet both. AVRIL is French for APRIL, and AVRIL is her legal name. But at about the age of 12, AVRIL, or APRIL as she goes by now, started to rebel. Its normal I guess. She went so far as to remove the V from the keyboard of her used typewriter and only used the key P.

So her school papers would describe a trip to Mammoth Cape, who knew Kentucky had a beach, or would discuss the local Honey farmers and their bee hipes. I had so many calls from her teachers, one of them even stopped by the house with a new typewriter, she was such a dear, the teacher I mean.

So I compromised and used the spelling AVPRIL.

MEL: Did that help?

AUDREY: No, not really. She still goes by APRIL. But I can rebel too.

(door opens and all others arrive, Mark, Avril, Guillaume, Simone, and Georges)

(Hugs and kisses)

AUDREY: Simone and Guillaume I am so happy that you're here. Let me show you to your room and we'll have a light lunch soon. April, can you show Georges where he will be sleeping?

AVRIL: You bet.

(Audrey, Simone, and Guillaume exit stage left)

MEL: Georges, I was telling your mother, I mean Audrey, how much you resemble Mark in these photos. Its even more striking in person.

MARK: Really? He resembles me? I think that you must have lost something in translation. Georges is Simone's son.

MEL: Yes, I remember now, That is what she told me. (To Avril), AVPRIL, that is a very unusual name. Did I get it right on the cake?

AVRIL: That depends on who you ask. I go by April.   Mom does her own thing, as long as its French. Come on Georges, I'll show you the room.

(Avril and Georges exit stage left).

MEL: Are they staying long?

MARK: They are leaving Sunday for New York, Guillaume has business there next week.

MEL: Its nice that they were able to come for Derby.

MARK: Yes, very much. We haven't seen each other in a very long time. Georges will be back for a month in July as part of the city's exchange program with Montpellier and will be staying with us.

MEL: So he will have already made a friend here.

MARK: Oh?

MEL: Yes, April. They seem to be hitting it off very well.

MARK: You think so? They've only just met an hour ago at the airport at Sandiford field. You may be right about them getting along, but you're incorrect about his stay. While Georges is with us in July, April will be spending the month with

Simone and Guillaume in France. She's the flip side of the exchange.

MEL: That's quite a coincidence.

MARK: Not really, they're the same age, almost exactly. Both were born in

MEL: April

MARK: April, yes. Being 19, they are adults, or at least college student adults. Well, I'll let you get back to doing whatever you need to do for lunch. I need to bring in their luggage (exits stage right)

MEL (looks at photos, shakes her head and gets to work)

End Act II scene 1

ACT II scene 2 (1 hour later, all but Mel seated at a table, Mel bringing dishes)

AVRIL: So, after your lost weekend in New York, what happened?

AUDREY: To tell the truth not very much. We came back and school started, so I went back to teaching and Dad was working very hard as well. And then a few months later, I found out that you were on the way. I lost touch with Guillaume and Simone, this was way before cellular phones and internet webs.   It wasn't until years later that I read about Guillaume's discovery and the sale of his company in Franco-Amerique. (to Guillaume)

Tu étais gêné, n'est-ce pas?

GUILLAUME: Oui, very embarrassed, even ashamed. Me voilà, j'étais venu à New York, m'être vanté avant de partir de Montpellier, que j'allais devenir riche and célèbre.

Quel horreur. Une fois de retour en France, je me suis rendu compte, grâce aux blagues sans cesse, de mon erreur. Croyez-moi, j'ai même songé à me suicider. On disait "Le père et le grand père, ils étaient des fous, mais il demande un couple pour se crever en Amérique, comme ils l'ont fait." Toute la ville nous a pris pour de véritables idiots.

Et puis, comme un coup de foudre, je me suis dit, tu as déjà créé le néant. Au lieu d'avoir fabriqué un parfum, j'avais créé ce qui est devenu une traitement pour l'angoisse, les maladies mentales, et de nombreuses blessures cérébrales.

Mel, this is very delicious (taking a bite of something). One learns by forgetting became my motto, ma devise. On apprend par l'oubli. And so my terrible defeat led to my discovery and my contribution to medical science. Oblivion is used by doctors in over 80 countries.

MEL: One learns by forgetting. Interesting thought. But you never determined exactly what happened during the weekend?

SIMONE: One says weekend, but tout cela s'est passé un Mercredi. That day, that Wednesday, is blank. It was a coupeur de courante, a blackout for us. We must have been drinking wine, been disturbed by the citywide blackout, it certainly made the newspapers, and somehow consumed the perfume.

AUDREY: One lost night, more or less, in your 20s is no big deal.

AVRIL: Thanks for the advice mom.

AUDREY;   That is not what I meant. I mean that..

AVRIL: Yes?

MARK: I think that what your mother is saying is that mixing unknown chemicals and alcohol has repercussions.

AVRIL: Like me?

MARK: Yes. But I would never describe you as a repercussion honey.

MEL: Georges, are you anticipating your upcoming stay here in Kentucky?

SIMONE: You may not like his answer.

GEORGES: I have been living as a partial American for years now. That is what my mother means.

MEL: A partial American? How so?

GEORGES: You will notice that my parents are enraptured by all things American. The language, the clothes, the music. I sometimes feel that I am living in an American outpost back in France.

MARK: Georges, this is fascinating. Tell us more.

SIMONE: You were telling us earlier about Avril, April, and the missing letters on the typewriter, the constant exposure to French. C'etait pareil pour Georges. Il s'appellait Georges Rican ou Georges D'Amerloc pour se moquer de nous.

GEORGES: I can speak by myself. America is everywhere now, it can be stifling. Malgré tout, la soi-disant culture américaine se répand partout au monde, comme une épidémie. Papa, je te donne donc ton prochain projet, arrêtes cette maladie.

AVRIL: Is that what you really think, that America is an epidemic?

GEORGES: Pardonnez-moi, j'exagère.

AVRIL: But that is your belief.

GEORGES: I am here, I will be here in July, to see for myself, the real America. Does such a place even exist? Peut-etre ont-ils torts, mes parents.

AVRIL: Cela arrive à nous tous.

GEORGES: Avoir tort?

AVRIL: Non, avoir des parents qui l'ont torts.

(All laugh except Mel, who looks to Audrey).

AUDREY: This is a good sign. Audrey and Georges have moved beyond attacking each other's country and have allied against the parents. There is hope for international relations after all.

MARK: I am still curious, Georges. What do you expect to see here?

GEORGES: I want to see how bad the food is (catches himself), not immediately of course, not this meal, this is very good. I would like to visit schools and see how students are taught and live, and to see how terrible American companies are.

MARK: I'm not sure how pleased or disappointed you will be, but you will see all of that in July. This exchange programs has been in existence for decades. Simone, your mother, may have had similar questions when she arrived.

SIMONE: No, not really (smiles). It was love at first sight.

GEORGES (breaking tension) I would also like to see this Mammoth Cape that Avril wrote of (smiles at Avril). Mais tu seras ailleurs.

MEL: We may not have a Mammoth Cape but we have mammoth horse races, today and tomorrow. And I just happen to have copies of the racing form.

GUILLAUME: Vous-avez le TABAC/PMU, ici?

AUDREY (laughs); We have tobacco for sure, but not the TABAC with paramutiel bettings that you do back home in France. (To Mel) : France has over 250 horse tracks.

MEL: Betting shops? I have one better. (Dances over to table to her purse from which she removes a large cellphone, and then dances back). With this, you can place your bets with me and I'll bring any winnings by later tonight.

GUILLAUME (picks up racing form and scans and begins speaking): Parier, Parier.

MEL: To bet?

GUILLAUME: Yes, to bet.

MEL: We have French jockeys in Louisville for all of the big races. One of them, Jean Cruguet won the triple crown in 1977. Hey, that was the year of the famous lost weekend in New York. This is a good omen. Pariez Guillaume.

End Act II scene 2

ACT II Scene 3 (a few hours later, table and its chairs removed)

(Parents are dressed for dinner, very bright derby jackets and ties for men, hats, pearls for ladies)

MEL :   So aren't you four ready for millionaire's row ! Or at least ready for Equus tonight.

GUILLAUME (looks to Mark) : Are you sure that this is appropriate wear ? It is....

éblouissant.

MARK :   That is the idea.

MEL : Every year, derby is like a lost weekend for the city. Its Mardi gras with horseshoes.

MARK : Guillaume, Mel is correct. And for us men, we know exactly what we'll be wearing each year, since I wouldn't wear this jacket to my own funeral otherwise.

MEL: You did very well at the track today Guillaume for not being there. I'll have your winnings for you when you return from Equus. (To Audrey). You have me blocked in, so I'll leave with you and the others, and will drop off the breakfast items later tonight.

AUDREY: You've been such a big help today Mel.

MEL: Like the shirt says, phone a buddie. Hey, I have a motto too, just like Guillaume.

GUILLAUME: Mark, do we have a few minutes before we leave for dinner? I'd like to show everyone something.

MARK: Sure, nothing in Louisville is further than 20 minutes away by car.

GEORGES: And by autobus?

MARK: You can measure that yourself in July. I'll admit that will be one of your disappointments.

GUILLAUME: Georges, va me chercher ma petite valise.   (Georges exits stage left)

AUDREY: Je commence à sentir un mystere. (Rubs the arm of Guillaume).

SIMONE (Rubs other arm of Guillaume).   Moi aussi. Cheri, c'est quoi ca? Une valise d'or?

GUILLAUME: Vous verrez.   Attendez un peu.

(George returns and passes small valise to Guillaume).

GUILLAUME: On apprend par l'oubli.

(Guillaume removes small rack with test tubes, two empty, two with liquid)

I am here to sell this to the American farmers. It is a easy and inexpensive way to verify parentage. This may be even purchased by those in the equine business. I have been working on this using students in the high school where I still teach a class twice a year.

SIMONE: Tes eleves sont des vaches et des cochons?

GEORGES: Si papa enseignait aux etats-unis, sans doute serait-ce le cas.

AVRIL (lightly punches Georges on shoulder): Soit poli.

(Guillaume passes a Q-tip to each of the others except Mel).

GUILLAUME: Je mets mon tampon dans cette éprouvette, et celui de Mark dans celle-là. J'y

ajoute une goutte d'agent de fixation (dips his and
Mark's samples into separate tubes and add a drop
of another liquid, disposes of q-tips) Audrey and
Simone? (extends hand) (Audrey collects and tries
to switch them, not clear if deliberate and passes
them to Guillaume who corrects the switch and dips
them in the tubes) En suite, j'y ajoute leurs
échantillons, suivi d'une goutte de la deuxième
solution. (Avril and Georges have approached and
are ready to pass him theirs. The solution has
turned blue)

AUDREY: Its blue. Is that good?

GUILLAUME: Yes, that is normal. (Takes and
dips in the last two samples and disposes of them .
drops in third fixer)

AUDREY: Its still blue.

GUILLAUME: Yes, that is normal. The process
will take a few hours to complete. Il faut cuver. It
must ferment in a sense. We will see the results
later. It will be pink, unless I've mixed the samples.
But you all saw that I did not.

MARK: I thought that we were going to dinner. Do we need to cancel if this will take hours?

GUILLAUME: No, we can leave at any time. Let me set this up (puts in on table near cake). We can share cake here at the house after dinner.

MEL: So what does the pink and blue mean, boy or girl?

GUILLAUME: No, not gender, but simply that the three samples are parents and child.

If I had used a sample from you Mel, instead of Simone or Audrey, the result would remain blue. This is being directed to the animal breeders and their clients who want to be assured of the lineage.

AUDREY: If this is for animals, why did we all just give samples? Guillaume, you used this on your students? Why?

GUILLAUME: Chère Audrey. I am not an American cowboy lassoing horses at a rodeo or chasing coyotes to collect their saliva. (smiles)

Students are a little easier to catch. But this process works for all mammals.

MARK: Guillaume, you've done it again, you will make another fortune with this. And you say that this works for all mammals; so this could be marketed for people?

GUILLAUME: Bien sûr, ça va de soi.

(Simone and Audrey exchange glance).

Mais assez de science. A table.

MEL (to Audrey): I'll drop off the breakfast items in a few hours.

AUDREY: Sure, that's fine.

All leave (stage right) except Avril and Georges.

20 seconds pass

Avril and Georges turn exit stage left

End ACT II scene 3

ACT II scene 4 (a few hours later)

(Avril and Georges enter stage left)

AVRIL: I do like that one song especically, Savoir Aimer. Thanks for bringing it over from France for me, Georges. Who is the artist again?

GEORGES: Florent Pagny. Il est vieux, mais il chante bien.

AVRIL: Its been over three and a half hours, they should be back soon. Three hours, more than enough time for the fermentation to have completed). (Goes to tubes and lifts it, not visible to audience until lifted). Look, its still blue. It must have failed.

GEORGES: (Comes over to look) Impossible.
Quand papa dit deux heures, il veut dire deux
heures. Tu le connaitras dès juillet. Papa est très
précis.

AVRIL (replaces tube to where cannot be seen by
audience and walks to center stage followed by
Georges): Then what does this mean? There was
no mixup in the samples, we both saw that. Only
your father is familiar with the entire process.

GEORGES: Both results are wrong, that can't be.
That would mean that we are both adopted.

AVRIL: Is this their way of telling us that we are
both adopted? They wait until we are together, both
of us over the age of 18. I thought it odd that we
have the same exact birthday.

GEORGES: Je trouve cette façon de nous
expliquer la vérité trop cruelle. Ce n'est pas
vraisemblable.

AVRIL: Yes, that would be a cruel way to break
the news, but one nevers understands how parents
think what they do.

AVRIL: A moins que nos parents nous ayons échangés à nos naissances. Non, c'est idiot. J'ai vu mon acte de naissance, je suis née à Louisville, et toi, Georges, ou es-tu né?

GEORGES: You were born here, and I was born in Montpellier. Aucun doute. – Attends, ton bonne m'a dit que je ressemblais à ton père.

AVRIL (bursts out laughing). Melanie is not our maid, she is a caterer, un traiteur.

She is also a busybody.

GEORGES: Yes, I saw her bizarre blouse.

AVRIL: C'est un jeu de mot en englais. She is a busy buddie, and a busybody, a gossip. Elle bavarde.

GEORGES: Ah, un corbeau.

AVRIL: Je ne peux pas pour autant dire ca. Elle bavarde.

(pause)

AVRIL: Où en sommes-nous avec nos théories?
Yes, where are we?

The test failed or is not yet complete? You say no

That we are both adopted or exchanged? That
makes no sense

That, that, our fathers are not our fathers?

GEORGES: That would mean that I am half
American and that....

AVRIL: And that I am half French.

GEORGES: I like both of your halfs (smiling)

AVRIL (small smack on Georges shoulder):
That's halves.

GEORGES: Have what?

AVRIL: Never mind.

Key noise in door and door opens. Mel enters with two bags.

MEL: Bonsoir. Audrey loaned me a key as we were leaving . I'm going to arrange some items for tomorrow's breakfast. You're going to have fun at the Derby tomorrow, take my advice and bet Silver Charm to win.

AVRIL: Ok. We're going to listen to some more music (Avril and Georges exit stage left)

(Mel arranges items on table with back to audience, French music (Savoir Aimer) heard offstage. This arrangement takes a few minutes.

Mel exits stage left.

Door opens and parents enter stage right, husbands are talkative, women are quiet.

Wives leave to remove coats and return 2/3 way through the discussion.)

MARK : Well thanks to that filly, Blushing K.d, and to Mel and her cell phone contact at the track, we had a wonderful meal at Equus. I'll need to get tips from her for tomorrow.

GUILLAUME: It even paid for a nice Bordeaux. The California wines are fine, but they can overwhelm the food.

(Husbands sit.)

Mark, do you remember that photograph of Muhammed Ali in the suite in New York?

MARK: Yes, why?

GUILLAUME: He said "The man who views the world at 50 the same as he did at 20 has wasted 30 years of his life"

MARK: That's very Zen.

GUILLAUME: Zen?

MARK: I mean deep, profound. But what does that mean? That I was wrong at 20 but correct at 50? Or the other way round? That one is never always correct? In my case I am not always wrong.

(Wives return and look at vials exchanging a blank look)

AUDREY: Not always, Mark, but often enough.

GUILLAUME: I think it means that is never one path for all occasions. One must adapt to new situations. Il faut s'accommode.

(Avril and Georges enter stage left).

AVRIL (looking at Guillaume): Georges and I noticed earlier that the vials are still blue. Your experiment did not seem to work.

GUILLAUME: Impossible!

AUDREY: April !

AVRIL: Then what does it mean? Are we adopted?

GUILLAUME: Qu'est-ce que tu dit? Adopté?

GEORGES: A moins que ce soit pire! Je suis américain?

SIMONE: Georges! Arrête!

AUDRY: April!

(Mel enters stage)

MEL: Ok good you're back. Time for cake.

MARK: Mel, this may not be the best time.

GEORGES (irritated but polite): Ce n'est pas l'heure de manger de gateau. Pas du tout.

GUILLAUME (to Georges): Américain? Adopté. Quelle blague est-ce?

MEL: Pas du tout. I learned that earlier today, didn't I Audrey ?

AUDREY (weakly). Yes.

MEL: Pas du tout. That means not at all, doesn't it? No cake at all ? Its always time for cake (next to cake, pushes wives away and raises tube rack slightly, audience cannot see it). Oh, look, Professor Guillaume, your experiment worked.

GEORGES (still excited). Non! Il a falli. It failed. Regardez (pointing to table).

MEL (raises tubes): See, they're pink. Just as you said that they would be.

(Wives and children open mouth).

GEORGES: Mais, mais elles etaient bleues.

GUILLAUME (checks watch): Rouge, bien sûr.
Apres quelques heures, elles deviendraient rouges.

AVRIL: Nous devions nous tromper. Il a fallu du
temps pour que le processus se termine. Thanks
Mrs. BUDIE, we must have checked too soon.

GUILLAUME: Georges, que disait-tu? Adopté?

GEORGES (recovering): It was only a joke. Avril
and I were tired of listening to music and came up
with a joke.

AUDREY: Not very funny. But cake can remedy
that.

MEL: Oh by the way, I've left your track winnings
on the end table, "le gueridon"?

SIMONE: Merci Melanie, vous etes vraiment merveilleuse. Vraiment merveilleuse.

MEL: April, let me cut you a slice of cake. I'll be sure to remove the V.

AVRIL: No, I'd like it without the P, my name is Avril. (Takes her slice and one for George and walk stage left). Lets eat this in your room, it's the American way.

GEORGES: A l'américaine. (George and Avril exit stage left).

MARK: I'm going to pass on cake, its been quite a day. Bonne nuit all. (kisses wives on cheeks and exits stage left).

GUILLAUME: Désolé mes chéries, je suis fatigue assui, moi. (kisses wives and exits stage left).

MEL: Well, its time for me to leave as well. Maybe Ed will want to practice some French tonight. Simone, I like what your husband said, On apprend par l'oubli. One learns by forgetting. I don't know what it means, but it sounds wise.

AUDREY; Do you know what else sounds wise? (Pause). Some wine. Please stay for another few minutes. (walks to wine area and returns with three glasses and distributes them. Pours some for red wine for Simone and then asks Melane) Melanie?

MEL: Well usually for Derby, one drinks a mint julep. But for me, since it is the run for the roses, I drink rosé. Je prends un rosé. (Mel takes wine glass. She walks to the test tubes, sets wine glass down, looks at Audrey and Simone, winks, picks up one tube in each hand and drinks them one after another, then replaces them. (She walks to the door and says before leaving) : Remember ladies : When you're too busy, call a buddy. (exits stage right).

(Audrey and Simone look at each other silently, then Audrey fills her glass, until now empty. Wives giggle, then clink glasses and drink.

SIMONE: Audrey, one more thing. Just to be clear, which is my bedroom tonight ? (both drink again)

FIN

A SIMPLY MISSING

By Gregory John Ferris

A SIMPLY MISSING

ONE

Later, when I began to gather my thoughts and materials for this book, I wondered if the events of those three weeks in the warmth of a Kentucky August had been nothing more than a humidity induced dream, chanted by cicadas .

The events seemed unlikely even to myself. Had any of it truly happened, except for the simple purchase of one man's memories in the form of a scrapbook, found by happenstance at neighborhood yard sale, and my few chance sightings of a mysterious woman.

These were trivial occurrences during what had been the most upsetting six months, in the past eighty years, for the entire planet. It had been a nightmare for hundreds of millions, the entirety of civilization had been threatened and suspended.

Arts, education, sports and other leisure had evaporated, replaced by the past time choice of either sheltering in place, or else march to destroy those remnants of human creativity that were still functioning. Perhaps all of these calamities were the result of the constantly predicted, yet delayed global warming. Violent riots with the ironic motive of protesting violence were only one manifestation of this recent most unusual of times.

Elsewhere crowds were noticeable by their absence. The radio was running its annual Christmas in July playlist, a valiant effort, but ultimately not up to the task.

Since March, COVID had been the topic of international concern, while parochially, in my corner of the spinning world, Lake Forest , the Button house had been the on-again off-again center of attention.

It had displaced the 2019 citywide obsession, the unexpected death of a local, retired police detective named Henry Percheron, or Perch to his many admirers.

Gossip was abundantly fertilized by the virus, to the point that neighbors who rarely acknowledged the existence of, let alone spoke to one another, succumbed to the need to huddle, to share, if not a fresh kill, then the prime cuts of hearsay and rumor. The more outlandish the claim, the more it was believed by the educated affluent, a not unreasonable reaction, as they had more to lose and more to fear.

The wife , Amy Button had died in the Spring, of an apparent heart attack. Her husband and 18 year old son, Sawyer, had left Louisville for months, leaving the house hands in the care of Sawyer's twenty year old girlfriend and neighbor, Kylie. Some neighbors speculated that Covid-19 was the actual cause of death and that authorities were hiding the truth. Others mentioned that Amy had been in good health and that as a former nurse, she would have recognized a cardiac problem. It was a mystery to which no one in authority paid the slightest attention.

The human buzz augmented that of the loud insects nesting in the surrounding trees and shrubs.

There was also the aunt, Muffin Button, who have arrived a few weeks before Amy's death, had made quite an impression on the men of the subdivision, and on their wives.

I met Muffin a few times, she was quite a talker. I'm a walker, so I was content to walk with her, leaving the majority of the discussion to her.

According to the infallible rumor mill, Muffin left town immediately after the funeral.

Sawyer and his father Damon had recently returned to Louisville and the rumor was that Sawyer and Kylie were engaged if not already married.

It was unheard of to have an eighteen year old marry, particularly in in Lake Forest, and to a not much older fellow resident. This behavior was still acceptable in Eastern Kentucky and third world countries where they continued to believe in gods and other myths, but not in these well-manicured back yards. Kylie's parents declined to provide any hors d'oeuvres in the form of information at all, let alone the main dish that their neighbors craved.

My story began in the most mundane of locations, a neighborhood yard sale.

I dislike yard sales, those rural and suburban euphemisms for rummage sales. They were depressing as a child, I sometimes wondered if somewhere in back, children were also for sale, clothes, books, and kid for one bargain price. Not in any trafficking way, but simply as another item that was one precious but whose presence was a constant reminder, 'What did I get this thing for?' Anyway, rummage sales are now yard sales and happiness reigns again.

I normally avoid such affairs, having satisfied my lifetime quota as a boy accompanying my mother to such weekly events.

She had recently passed away after having nearly attained the century mark. I must have been reflecting on her missed achievement as I passed the yard sale and was subconsciously compelled to stop and browse.

Such sales were held once or twice per year in Lake Forest, and this one had likely been grandfathered in, with social distancing and masks mandated here as they were elsewhere. This one was well attended, for there was still little else to do that involved both the sun and human contact.

Chinese constructed toys, Bangladeshi sewn clothes, and books by a motley collection of nationalities constituted the bulk of the material on display. Other than the countries of origin, it was little different from those I had been dragged to a half century earlier.

A homeowner whom I did not know, but who evidently recognized me, called out to me. I had already passed by his offerings, but he called again, and motioned me over.

"I was hoping that you would stop by," he said excitedly.

"Hello."

"I'm Mark, and that is my wife Audrey over there by the lamps. You are the local writer, aren't you?"

"I write sometimes," I replied noncommittally.

"I thought so. I have just the thing for you", he boasted, pulling out a large book from a bag that lay on the grass beside the table. "Have a look at this."

I took the offered object and studied it. It was more of a large scrapbook or a photo album than an actual book. I turned a few pages, each with a photo of one person, their name below it, a few scribbled notes in the same hand, and that was about it.

"That is a Lake Forest yard original, I can provide provenance."

"Provenance on a scrapbook?" I asked good-naturedly.

"What you have in your hands in the Percheron death book."

"Oh? I never heard of it," I responded as I set it down.

"Its photographs of some, if not all of the murder victims on whose cases Detective Percheron worked. And some of his handwritten notes. I thought that it might be the start of his memoirs, or it was the partner to a manuscript. That is why I've kept it. It's been a year, during which time I was wondering if there had been a companion dossier that someone else had bought. I guess not. This is it, a local holy grail."

"Mark must be in sales," I thought. "Or he likes to drink. Probably both," I concluded.

"Since you like to write, I thought that perhaps you might be able to do something with this. Its only $50."

If someone had offered him $20 at that moment, he'd have sold it in a heartbeat. As it was, a photo book of clothed strangers had little appeal to one and all.

I made a mistake at that moment and pursued the conversation. "What would I do with it?"

"Whatever it is that you do. You might be able convert it in a local historical human interest, multicultural, immigrant piece."

He strung the words together like multiple lures on a fishing line, and I bit.

"Yeah, that should be easy enough". I handed over less than Mark's asking price and more than it was worth. Both of us felt cheated as I turned and began to leave.

I spun back and asked, "Did you know him well?"

"Detective Percheron? No, not well. Even after he retired I did not see much of him. I caught sight of him with one of the staff from Brady Funeral Home, Martin Aikens. He's retired too. You'll notice the Brady Funeral notation on a few of the pictures in the book. Aikens might be a person to start with." Mark likely thought this last suggestion worth an agency fee at some future time.

"Great," I thought, "Retirees, funeral homes, and murder victims, and Halloween just weeks away. This has all the ingredients of a zero sales book. Trick or trick, no treat likely".

"I followed the case, Percheron's murder," Mark added in response to my puzzled look.

I was already regretting my purchase.

"You must remember, he was murdered as well, Derby last year."

It was the last Derby, for this year's race had been postponed until Labor Day weekend.

So much had transpired recently. Here it was, 16 months since the last big blowout in Louisville, and there was no hint of similar happiness in the foreseeable future.

I did recall that Percheron had been murdered. Various scandals had followed, and the accused killer had died before trial.

Maybe all of this pain and sorrow could, with a little luck, be converted into something. But what, exactly? Not a scrapbook over spiced with adjectives, but an entertaining story. A book, one true and useful.

The day looked a little brighter.

TWO

"You have no children, Mrs. Favor?" Detective Percheron asked the bruised woman lying in a hospital bed in Baptist East hospital. He had been talking to her for a few minutes at the behest of one of the on duty nurses.

"The nurses seem see more pain that I do," he mused.

In a few minutes he would be speaking with the family of the gunshot victim who had died 30 minutes ago in the nearby emergency room. In the interim, he was doing the nurse a favor. "Funny," he thought,"a favor for a Favor."

"No, detective, I have no children. I won't, not to Bruce."

Percheron, Perch to his friends, knew that he had only few moments to advise the woman, an attractive 30ish blonde. That was what the nurse had sent him to do, what he himself felt was part of his serve and protect ethos, and undoubtedly what this abused wife needed to hear. He was equally positive that she would ignore his blunt suggestion.

"Mrs. Favor, go. Take what you can carry and leave. As soon as you can, but soon. Here, take this card, it is for a shelter."

"A battered women's shelter?"

"Yes," he said flatly. He passed a second card to her. "And this is another".

"This one is just a phone number".

"It is low profile, private."

"Does that mean expensive?"

"There is no cost. It is private so they don't advertise. Husbands and boyfriends can be crafty as well as nasty. So they are very low key."

"No address?"

"They move from time to time. Honestly, I do not know where they are located today. If you call them, use my name.

They may call me to doublecheck or they may have you come right away and they will call me later."

"I see," Mrs. Favor said.

"When you decide to go, don't waste time packing. Take the minimum and leave. Frankly, these shelters are not luxurious hotels. They are little more than hostels, where everyone, even those for whom the shelter exists, has to contribute to make a go of it. It's not the Seelbach."

"I need to know, is it safe?"

"It's safer, Mrs. Favor."

"Please, just Sharon, detective. I don't consider myself a Missus today, simply a missing."

"The shelter is safer. No place is safe."

"Not even with you?"

"Not even with me." Her plea was not the first time he had heard it. People had unrealistic expectations of policeman. He regretted having to disappoint them.

"Is that a possibility?"

"No." Percheron paused. "I'm sorry, but"

"I'm the one who is sorry. This is all so new, and sudden."

"Be thankful for that."

The nurse entered the room and informed Perch that the family of the deceased shooting victim had arrived. The detective left, having delivered a message of warning, seasoned with hope. For the family of the young, dead, gunshot victim, the message would be one hundred percent bitter.

THREE

I was stopped at a red light in my small hometown on Middletown, one of several independent cities within the confines of Louisville, Kentucky. A flatbed loaded with brand new fire hydrants, each with an eight foot extension of black pipe, crossed from my right to my left, then turned east on Shelbyville road.

It was an unusual sight. Obviously fire hydrants are fabricated somewhere and delivered to where they are installed, but like many of the components of modern life, they are rarely noted, nor, as in this case, are they detected in transit.

I surmised that this load was destined to one of the new housing developments that were rapidly replacing the former farms that stretched to the eastern extent of the Louisville/Jefferson County line.

As the truck past, I glimpsed the woman for the first time.

She was too well dressed for a homeless woman, even a debutante sans abri.

A sleeveless, yellow summer dress, cotton, medium length blonde hair, flats, the impression was of a 30ish woman on her way to a neighborhood barbecue, where she would treat herself to a raspberry martini. Or perhaps she intended to pass the afternoon with friends, playing Bridge or mahjong.

But there was something out of place with my casting her in such a role.

It was the sheer number of small, colorful bags, that she wore, shouldered and carried.

It was a motley, inexpensive collection. They appeared to contain no packages or wrapped gifts, nor were the bags themselves adorned with designer logos.

Sitting at the long traffic light as she trod on, I counted at least seven. Extended traffic lights have become my time for reflection, as they offer a respite between successive internet bombardments. Attacks that destroy by sapping immediacy from real life and replace it with a plasma for faux existence.

"Who was she?" I wondered.

I sensed that she was both determined to advance, compelled to reach some destination, yet unsure whether she was moving in the correct direction. Was she herself confident in her path?

I doubted it. I sighed and sent a silent, worthless wish on her behalf to wherever it was supposed to go. In that regard, we were similarly confused in our navigation. Whose destination was the less meaningful, hers or mine?

She was not shaking, yet I sensed that inside she was vibrating madly, her poise maintained but unstable and teetering, on the verge of shattering.

It was visible in her blue eyes tinted with fear.

I took it as a healthy sign. If she still harbored trepidation, then crazy had not assumed complete command.

In a time when riots and virus contended for YouTube eyeballs, if not for Facebook likes, her oddity raised little alarm. It was tolerated and although noticed, her presence had a calming effect, psychosis such as hers were a reminder of a normal past, before the new normal present. What had been feared as mild insanity was now classified as a trivial problem on the periphery. She was a manageable intrusion in a world filled with actual danger.

None of the other drivers were paying the slightest attention to the woman.

The light blinked from red to green, and I continued west. I thought no more of her.

FOUR

Percheron regretted not having spoken with Sharon's husband, Bruce, in the hospital, but he had more pressing matters to attend. The husband had not shown up to see Sharon until the following day, so Percheron had missed nothing by not waiting.

He had not received a phone call from either of the two shelters that he had recommended to the Favor woman. Perch was not alarmed at this lack of contact. Experience taught him that among the abused fear can overcome their desire to escape and they end up as no shows. Regardless, he would follow up with her.

Two days later, the detective drove to the Favor residence, a small house with a tiny back yard, set on one of the numerous side streets that extended from Bardstown road.

Mr. Favor was sitting on a metal chair on the front porch, listening to the radio. The husband was drinking a lemonade, the glass was nearly empty, and so much condensation was spread on the round glass table that the glass could have had a slow leak. Cicadas were singing, as if they were cheering the sports action that could be heard coming from the radio. It was a deceptively peaceful image.

Percheron, announced himself and presented his badge, asking permission before opening the chain link fence and ascending the few concrete steps. He noticed that there was only one chair on the porch.

"Is your wife at home, Mr. Favor?"

"What's this about? Are you here about her accident?"

"No, I'm not. I wasn't aware that there was an accident investigation. I met your wife for a few minutes the other evening at Baptist East, during another case that I'm working. I'm with homicide."

Favor was not fat, nor thin, but square. He was singularly lacking in parts that were supposed to round. He was dressed in bluish gray shorts and a matching T shirt. He resembled nothing so much as a frog transformed into an amphibian's ideal of a prince, and a middle aged one at that. His manner was that of a toad and he was perfect in all the ways that there were to be cast as a human frog in a horrible fairytale.

"Do homicide investigators handle attempted murder cases?"

"Sometimes. I thought that you said it was an accident?"

"I am referring to your other case, the one at the hospital."

"That victim died. He was shot, likely for no reason."

"Someone shot this person without cause. Surely, there must be a reason."

"No, I think that he reached a point that he thought he could and furthermore that he could get away with it. In his mind it was little different than running a red light on a Sunday morning. There was no reason, but a motive. Arrogance, evil, who knows?"

"Don't you?"

"People surrender to bad intentions. I'm amazed that the majority of people are as honest as they are."

"If they weren't then you couldn't keep up?"

"Otherwise society would not have police."

"You can't kill everyone."

"Some try."

"That came out other than I intended. Everyone can't kill someone."

"I suppose that you're right."

"I must be correct. If not, there would be no humans remaining. You did say that your name is Percheron? I remember your name from the news. Percheron, they call you Perch."

Percheron ignored the comment.

"I've wished that the percentage of killers was lower than it is."

"What would you do then? For a job, that is?"

"I'd manage. I'm not holding my breath. My wishes rarely come true."

"I hear that your hunches do. You're the boy wonder cop, I seen your picture in the C-J a few times. What are you doing here? No one is dead in this house."

"That's good to hear, Mr. Favor. I could use a day off."

"With all of these senseless killings, why are you here?"

"To talk to Mrs. Favor, about this other case."

"Is she a suspect? Did she kill someone? Sharon, come here. What is this all about?"

Sharon exited from the house onto the porch, carrying a full glass of lemonade. Her husband took it from her and passed her its now empty companion.

"Oh! Hello Detective."

"What is this about, detective. Who's dead? Sharon, did you kill someone? Are you planning to."

"It is nothing of the sort, Mr. Favor. As I mentioned a few moments ago, I met Mrs. Favor the hospital a couple of days ago. She was there when the family and friends of a shooting victim was also there."

"Percheron turned to Sharon. I thought that perhaps you saw or heard something that might have bearing on my investigation."

"Is this one of your hunches? Is it true that you think like a criminal?"

"I hope not," Percheron replied with a good natured smile.

"Do you try to get inside the murderer's head?"

"Sometimes, but that is a very unpleasant place. Often, it is the opposite."

"The killers attempt to get into your head?"

Sharon's head moved from side to side watching the conversation, her right hand wet from the remnants of condensation.

"They do, but too late. They are arrested by that time."

"So what are you saying?" Sharon asked quietly

Percheron turned his gaze to the woman.

"I try to understand the victim."

Sharon spoke again.

"Why? Is their death their fault? Do they bring it on themselves?"

Percheron shifted his attention to the man.

"Would it be ok if Mrs. Favor and I continued this interview privately? This is an ongoing investigation. It will only take a few minutes. We can step into the house, or"

"No, stay here. I'll wait inside."

Bruce left, ignoring his wife's unspoken request to take the empty glass with him. Percheron began to speak but Sharon cut him off.

"I appreciate your concern, but we both know that I had no contact with anyone in the hospital other than doctors, nurses, and you."

"No, I guess that you didn't. Alright, I am positive that you have nothing to help me. I used the coincidence of your presence at the hospital as a pretext to speak with you again. You cannot assist me, but maybe I can help you."

Sharon remained silent.

"I came to remind you about the shelter. You were in shock the last time we spoke."

"No, I wasn't."

"You were. You may still be in shock."

"I still have the cards that you handed to me."

"They are not a magic potent sitting in your purse. But they could be if you use them."

"You could have telephoned."

"I wanted to make an impression on your husband."

"I've found that trying to impress Bruce has a tendency to backfire."

"So I should not have stopped by?"

"Probably not. It might not matter either way." She paused and then continued.

"My question about victims bringing their death on themselves. You didn't answer it."

"Some of the nasty victims do bring it on themselves."

"Nasty victims?"

"Those victims who in slightly different circumstances, would themselves be the upright killers instead of lying in the morgue."

"And the other, non-nasty victims?"

"The innocents? Through naiveté, kindness, inexperience,they take actions that result in their death, or they avoid actions that could have extended their lives."

"Oh."

I'm here as a courtesy.

"Did you notice the look on Bruce's face when he thought that I might be a murder, or do you say murderess in your business?"

Percheron followed Sharon's attempt to lighten the mood.

"Not that I've heard. We leave lurid to the press. We write nonfiction, they specialize in fiction and horror. If our roles were reversed, they would be the ones to require public funding."

Sharon detoured back to the detective's visit.

"Courtesy to me?"

"To both you are your husband. I've seen cases before"

"Is that what I am, a case?"

"Yes. Your case, such as it is now will be closed by the hospital. You claim that your injury was an accident. I'm not a doctor, I am not an attorney. I am not a psychologist."

"Are you all three in one?"

"Maybe I am. You should know that our meeting was not an accident. One of the nurses in attendance suggested that I check on you that day at the hospital."

"Is she your girlfriend?"

"More or less."

"That sounds vaguely romantic."

"She would agree. She is your friend too."

"I don't even know her, I can't remember her name."

"Nurses have many friends, you'd call them patients. She was concerned about you. So am I. Mrs. Favor, you aren't taking this seriously."

"Taking what seriously?"

"Humor has its place, and so does fantasy. But not today, not here, not for you."

"I'm sorry, I understand that you are trying to help."

"When I said that your case will be closed by the hospital I was going to warn you that I am worried about you becoming one of my cases."

"You're frightening me, detective."

"That is not my intention."

"No?"

"You should already be frightened, and not by me. I've seen this pattern," Percheron said calmly, holding up a hand to stop her objection.

"One occurrence is not a pattern."

"Is that your defense? Was it only the one? If so you are very fortunate. But there will be more."

"So you suggest that I leave."

"These situations don't end well. There is going to be a crash, it's up to you to reduce the severity of the impact. I am sorry, Mrs. Favor."

"Please call me Sharon."

"I hope to never call you Sharon, Mrs. Favor."

"I see. No, frankly I don't see. It's rude to be so formal. Why won't you call me Sharon?"

Perch had worked a few similar assignments, where circumstances had arranged themselves such that he saw the victim both before and after their death. He did not like such cases.

"I am only on a first name basis with those whose murders I am trying to solve. It helps me then, before it would act only as a distraction."

Percheron turned and descended the three concrete steps, opened the chain link gate, walked through and closed it.

He glanced backward to see if the woman was still there, for she had said nothing in response to his final words. She was silently holding the glass, condensate seeping between her fingers, like cold tears from closed eyelids.

FIVE

It was the late detective Percheron's private book of the dead, with photographs of the victims arranged chronologically. Names of funeral homes, presumably the one that had conducted the service, were next to each photo which I speculated that the family had provided.

Had each successful case brought him a modicum of satisfaction, hope that bringing each killer to account prevented other, future deaths.?

Did these hundreds sacrificed to violence bear witness to the millions more fortunate? Was the book not merely a catalog of the dead but, like an old photographic negative, did it obscure in its shadow the light of the still living?

I opened Percheron's photo book and began turning the pages. So many killings in our peaceful town, so many and yet we ranked low nationwide. Photo after photo, each face looking back, unaware that their future was so limited. Their brief lives captured in what would become their last moment, for this was the image saved for posterity. This is how they would be remembered by the man who was tasked with capturing their murderer. The click of the shutter marked the beginning of their final lap. A shiver ran down my spine, and I swore to never again have my photo taken.

I had paused flipping pages, and when I looked down again, I saw a photo that struck me instantly as being familiar. Who was it? No, it can't be. This is the woman whom I had seen yesterday, on Shelbyville road, near Brady Funeral home. Well, she was near many other places too, I corrected myself, Thornton's, and dry cleaners, and gas stations, and well, just about every business imaginable.

Printed beneath her photo, was a name; Mrs. Sharon Favor.

She had medium length blonde hair. I estimated her age at anywhere from the late 20's to the mid-30's. She regarded the camera seriously but with a hint of a smile. This may have an important occasion and she wanted to mark it appropriately. She was wearing a sleeveless yellow summer dress. Too young to die, I thought. A lie.

SIX

Sharon had called the number of the private shelter, they had told her come immediately. She wrote down the address, and realized that it would take several bus transfers to reach that part of town.

The detective had advised her to take only what she needed.

Take what you need, leave the rest and what she took were household items, some food , cleaning supplies, a few clothes. No furs, no jewelry; she had none to take. She carried all in a random selection of bags, straw, plastic , a brown paper sack with handles.

It was a hurriedly filled assortment that marked her to a trained eye as a refugee.

In her home, any hope she had of achieving any of her lifelong goals was fading, as she felt herself shrinking, disappearing into nothingness

In the small home off Bardstown road, her time was running out, yet experience had deterred her from action. She had exchanged courage for prudence years ago, a costume change she regretted ever since.

Today she was beginning anew.

She was happy for the first time in many years.

SEVEN

Funeral homes keep excellent records. It had proven difficult to do research with local protests and government offices closures, and the information for which I was searching was not online. I called the Brady Funeral home, and after speaking with the director about Sharon Favor and several other names from the dead book, he took my number and indicated that I would hear something one way or another.

So it was that the next day, I found myself sitting on the patio of the reopened Starbucks across from Kroger's, discussing events of more than twenty years previous with a retired undertaker, one Martin Aikens.

After a few pleasantries, he began telling me a story about a dog.

"I remember Smitty, he was our neighbor's dog, a beagle who lived outside in his own pen. This was a different time, an old world in some ways.

Few people had pets, it was a working class neighborhood, maybe kids were considered shared pets, eliminating the need for four-legged animals.

So a dog was somewhat special, he was a shared pet for us kids.

Anyway, one day, Smitty was hit by a car. While the owner, the father of our friend Robbie, was doing whatever he needed to do, me and my friend, Rat, that's a nickname, isn't it, and another friend, Becky, we were all of us about seven or eight years of age, time really does fly. Rat, and Becky and me, we had our spur of the moment conference. Impromptu you might say.

I remember hearing the world vet mentioned. Let me tell you, that was a magical word, a prayer and a curse. None of us had ever seen a real veterinarian, they were for rich people and for farmers. We were neither, by that I mean the adults. It was very blue collar. If Smitty needed a vet, well, he was done for."

I nodded my head to indicate that I was following the rambling story, maybe like how Smitty would follow the scent of a rabbit.

"The three of us ran to our homes and returned to Robbie's house, almost before we had left. I could really run back then. Smitty was wrapped in a blanket and Robbie's dad, Mr. Hudans, was putting the dog into the back seat. There was a rifle, a .22 I think, in the front seat."

"I see," I said solemnly, but it turned out that I did not. Aikens continued recounting his epic.

"When he saw us, he paused, which provided us the opportunity to approach him. We offered him the three piggy banks that we had retrieved from our rooms. I remember distinctly that Becky's was pink ceramic. Oddly I can't recall mine and Rat. I guess the color of two piggy banks is not important all these years later."

"Probably not," I agreed.

"Mr. Hudans stared at us strangely. And then something unexpected happened."

I said nothing, sure that Aikens would tell me in his way, and at his pace.

"He leaned into the car, and moved the rifle onto the floor in the back. He then inverted each bank in turn, removed the plug, and poured a handful of coins, removed a dime and replaced the remaining money and base plug, and then returned our banks to us.

I recall his words as if it were yesterday. Yeah, that should cover the vet bill. You kids think of everything."

He then told Robbie to hop in the front and off they went."

Aikens took a sip of his tea, and commented, "This was better before COVID." He took another sip, swallowed, and went on speaking.

"Smitty recovered. It was hilarious seeing a dog in a rear leg cast, and he lived for many more years.

Mr. Hudans was wise enough to never return our dimes directly, but he more than compensated us with ice cream, a lesson, and of course the return of the neighborhood celebrity pet."

"That is a wonderful story," I said when it was clear that Aikens was through with the tale.

"I like it a lot, it brings back good memories. But that is not why I told it to you."

"Oh?"

"I wanted to see if you had the patience to listen without interrupting. I needed to see if you were open to possibly wasting your time on an old man that might not be credible. You pass the test. My former partner at Brady's told me that you wanted to speak to me about some of my work from years ago. He didn't provide any details."

"I don't know where to begin, Mr. Aikens."

"I suppose that you want to talk about ghosts."

His directness took me by surprise.

"I see that you have Percheron's image book with you. You are not in law enforcement, so it's not about a new or old case, you did not brag about being a reporter, so again it's not about a case."

"But why a ghost?"

"Why not a ghost? I have met all sorts of people in my career, and out of necessity and a dash of curiosity I looked into various beliefs. I talked to many of the religious and some what you might even call mystics or psychics.

It's rare, but a ghost can be traumatized, and in a way, come back to what we could mistake for life. Hate and fear can be as immortal as love. Which ghost did you see?"

Aikens made it so easy to present my case, all the hard lifting, convincing another human that I was not mad, had been performed with his words, "Which one did you see?"

I opened the book to Sharon Favor's page.

"I'm not surprised."

"I sure as hell was."

"Sharon is disoriented. This is where Percheron's presence, his"

"Aura?"

"That has becoming a term of derision so I won't use it. The detective's scent, as it were, is at its strongest here, where he lived the longest. It is here that he ate, slept, in short where he existed. But Sharon is following clues in her own darkness where the few familiar items are like signs written in a foreign language. She is searching for one face, unaware that its owner is as dead as she."

"Don't they all know each other over there?" I asked as a child might.

"They are buried in different cemeteries. I know that for a fact."

"Does that explain her obvious lack of knowledge about Percheron?"

This conversation was beyond odd, and I wondered for a moment if somehow the coffee had gone bad sitting for so long, and now possessed a hallucinogenic component.

"I admit to having no clue about the physics of this world, let alone the next one. Apparently, she was drawn to the places where Perch had recently passed the majority of his time recently, where his scent so to speak was concentrated, in Middletown and Lake Forest. This is a guess, it fits the facts as you have presented them. Whether it explains what happened, like I said, who knows?"

"Did Percheron believe in this stuff?" I queried.

"No, I don't believe that he did. He had consulted a psychic once on a case, but I think that was for show, or out of desperation. Ironically, I think the book proves my point about his scepticism. If he believed in ghosts, then there is no need to retain photographs as reminders of a person's existence. Creating such a memorial is only required if they are truly gone. Otherwise its superfluous."

I directed the conversation back to Sharon Favor.

"She is lost in a sort of time fog?" I asked, feeling foolish. I was glad that social distancing prevented any of the other customers from eavesdropping

"Yes, her world has changed, and it is impossible for her to recover it. I don't intend to be funny, but there are disadvantages to being dead."

I was reminded again of how the snapshots of the dead were frozen points in time, never to be relived.

"And I thought that I was confused. This is all very spooky, voodooish. Is this some strange religion?"

"Religion is useful in the abstract, like Santa Claus."

He paused for a long moment.

"You should go visit her," he said, jotting down the name of a cemetery on my Starbuck's receipt.

As I stood to leave, Martin Aikens pulled out his wallet, and took from it an old photograph, which he presented for my review. It was in color, and was a photo of six or so kids, with pride of place in front of them taken by a beagle with a cast on one back leg.

EIGHT

Bruce didn't drink alcohol, so he contented himself with a fresh glass of lemonade. It's too bad that Sharon wasn't around to make him one of hers, but then he would not be toasting her absence if she was.

"That is a genuine paradox," he said aloud to himself.

"No booze for me," he congratulated himself silently.

"I'm not a bad sort, not a bad husband. Alcohol would have made me abusive. A drunk would have killed her so much earlier, for no reason. Killing was so easy, anyone could manage it.

My mind is not muddled, not with booze.

That cop thought that he could help Sharon. He only made things worse.. And now he wants to pin the blame on me.

My mind is wonderfully clear. But before, it was like a plume of dust trailing a speeding car down a dry unpaved farm road. When I stopped, the dust formed itself into a cloud that caught and enveloped me. It muddled my thinking and obscured the truth for a while.

I've learned my lesson, don't stop.

'Smart men can be such asses. They have no off switch, or they have one that can't bring themselves to flip it.'

I remember Sharon telling me that once. Well, honey I flipped the off switch, but it was yours, not mine.

I planned it well, it was very logical. I almost reconsidered, but she would not have changed. I was content. If Sharon wasn't satisfied that was not my fault.

I'm not too timid to state the obvious. Too many husbands are. They are weaklings."

Bruce regarded the handful of invoices in his hand. Sharon's bruises had still not healed when she was killed, and it was a morbid coincidence that both hospital and funeral home bills had arrived simultaneously.

She had been dead for nearly two weeks and the postman continued to deposit unwanted reminders of her in Bruce's mail box. The only remnant he desired had still not arrived. He was aniouxs for the check not yet received from the life insurance company.

"Will I soon have legal bills as well? Do they forward mail to prison?

That cop is after me, there is no doubt. If Percheron gets me, I, will be broke, in prison for most of the remainder of my life, all because I took control, as a good husband should."

Bruce Favor enjoyed the hunt. Being the quarry was alright with him, he was bound by nothing.

In this matchup, he was both prey and predator. His mentality was not that of a creature evolved to flee. Percheron's badge was not a protective shield, on the contrary, it was a weighted handicap, a legally enforced constraint on the detective's actions. He had no such restriction, his was complete freedom of movement.

This cop might be the young prince of LPD, but he answered to a higher power, himself.

He had called God once with a simple question, "Do we have a bargain?"

The expected answer had arrived – silence.

Bruce took that as yes or no, as subsequent circumstances required. It was a universal green light, thank God, he chuckled to himself. He would discover soon if his get out of jail card was still valid. Life was too long not to have fun, and he was the sole judge of what constituted fun. God's silence confirmed that it was ok, and really, who was he to thwart God's will?

"I was clever with the two cars, in two separate parking garages. And one of them so near to the central police station. That was a masterpiece," he reflected, sipping more lemonade.

"Sharon's was better," he admitted, setting the glass down.

"The old car is gone, long gone, probably on its way to China."

Favor had driven it from the parking garage to the junkyard a few days ago.

"The car is crushed now, just like Sharon."

He had saved the stolen Indiana plate and kept it in his workshop, as a trophy and as his own private joke.

NINE

2020 was a misnamed year. All was unclear, unhealthy, unperceivable. And now, as August began to show signs of Fall, with maybe back to school sales, and the closure of only partially open swimming pools, this year's theatrical production was preparing its next costume change. From green, to yellow, and then to red, nature's own traffic light pattern, mirroring the human one that had set me on my own theater of the absurd.

I sat in my home trying to make sense of Martin Aiken's theory.

Maybe this man was brilliant and I was too dull to understand it, or maybe his mind was the one unsharpened by years of exposure to embalming chemicals.

It can be impossible to distinguish between the image and its reflection. When I raise my left hand, is that what I am doing, or am I the reflection of a man raising his right hand?

I was left with the sensation that in attempting to refute his theory I had instead confirmed it.

Back home, it was a ridiculous fantasy. Ghosts from nearly 25 years ago walking the streets of Middletown Kentucky in broad daylight, for some reason visible only to me?

That was strange. To have a total stranger propose it to me with no prompting was bizarre.

Inside my house, it was all so distant. And to be sure, I had only seen this woman once, for a matter of two minutes at most. Yet she had occupied my thoughts since that chance encounter. Aiken's acceptance of my own private ghost might only confirm that insanity was not unique to me.

I don't understand how this world functions and I've been in it, well, my entire life.

I'm still trying to get the hang of this existence, and it does not help that it keeps on changing. Why on Earth, or off Earth to be precise, would I be expected to have a clue to some other world? Was I still on this planet, or was it me that was out of phase in some new existence?

Since March, I had reverted to living like a medieval man, rarely venturing more than a few miles from my home. I had as excuse the universal closures, but had as a reason simply being content with my place in my time in life. I had my 21 century amenities, I cocooned myself waiting for some miracle to occur and I don't mean a vaccine, but something exciting, more exciting than a pandemic. There was no moat surrounding my village, no wall, so there was no defense against the disease. Nor it turned out, against the most unusual of occurrences in this most odd of times.

I had acquired the dead man's book of the dead, based on a whim and in response to peer pressure. I felt somewhat dead myself. My expectations for the book had been rock bottom, undoubtedly it would be worthless drivel, disorganized, amateurish, in brief, totally in sync with my own recent work.

Who knew? Could I learn something from a man that I did not know. We might become acquaintances, friends in a way, and a dead friend was better than none at all.

If Aikens were correct in all of this hocus-pocus, then why was it Sharon and not Percheron himself who had returned? After all, it was his book.

I considered either opening a beer or going for a walk. I chose the latter.

I missed the handful of walks that I had taken with Muffin Button, the aunt of the husband of Amy Button, the former nurse who had died under mysterious circumstances that the police refused to investigate. Would she be coming back as a ghost too? I laughed at the silliness of my thought.

I was lost in a collage of ideas, counter-ideas, thoughts for and against, and I was nearly upon her as we met on the sidewalk leading from Lake Forest to Shelbyville road.

It was her, Sharon!

It was the same woman, the same dress, the same shoes not designed for long walks, the same bags. As we passed each other, and pass we did, for I was too amazed to stop or speak, I glanced down and saw cleaning supplies in one of the open top bags that she held in her left hand.

I was tempted to stop, to turn around, to call out, to approach her. I commanded myself to turn round and snap a photo of her, instead I disobeyed and walked on like Lot.

I would see her on my return. It was only another three or four minutes to Shelbyville Road . Once there, I touched the side of the brick gate like a public mezuzah. The gate was solid, it was brick, it was real. I was not dreaming.

I retraced my steps, expecting to cross paths again with the woman. It was unnerving, did my not passing her again indicate that she lived in the neighborhood? If she had been the ghostly Sharon, surely she would have stopped me? But Aikens believed that she was not looking for me, but for Percheron. I could not win this otherworldly argument with myself.

Maybe this was just one of the country's countless homeless, a woman living within the long, narrow band of trees that bordered the large fields on either side of the parkway? Or was Sharon getting closer and closer to my home? I hurried my pace, uncertain as to which outcome I preferred less.

TEN

You the reader may find this tract difficult to follow, but it is solely because you also have an essential role in this story, namely to assign it meaning and grant acceptance that I am not completely mad.

Was that why Sharon returned? Was it to ask for the help that she had once declined? Had she come to me in the stead of Percheron? Was she unable to contact him directly in whatever afterlife they inhabited? Or had he sent her to me, to act as his ignorant agent drafted to perform so unknown task? Why did she not stop, when we passed by, a few feet from one another on my walk?

I was startled, and yes, fearful. I am confused, having no idea of how to answer my own questions. I recount what I saw and experienced, or to the sceptics among you, what I believe that I saw and experienced.

I saw Sharon twice in person but never in flesh and blood. I learned recently that her husband was convicted of her murder. Her inclusion in the dead book was proof of her murder, I was now aware of the identity of her murderer.

Writing a novel is a hard, difficult lie. I suspect that it must be the same for murder. You must keep track of each previous falsehood, and invariably you will forget one and the entire structure will collapse, and work must begin anew. The most skilled fabricator will find himself or herself standing alone, clutching handfuls of verbal yarn that would not support the overwhelming mass of deceit. So it was in the Favor murder.

Life is strange. We are each entitled to our own reality in it.. Whether you judge this account credible or delusional, the ramblings of a man too long in confinement, both compulsory and voluntary, I will content myself with its truth.

Tomorrow I will go visit the grave of Sharon Favor. I don't expect to find any answers there, but neither am I am prepared to accept any more questions.

ELEVEN

Percheron and his colleague Castorina Ertras had been working the Favor murder for 10 days now.

After having attended the funeral, spoken to the bereaved and interviewed friends, family and neighbors, they had settled on two prime suspects: Bruce Favor, and any one driving an old, dark, Honda accord with an Indiana license plate ending in 117.

Percheron had discovered that Favor had withdrawn 400 dollars and then another 200 dollars from an ATM four days before the murder.

"Let's assume that Favor killed Sharon himself. He is a DIY personality, I noticed the tool shed in his back yard. I don't think that he would outsource anything that he could accomplish himself.

"He could have bought a beater car, like the one reported by the witness to the hit and run."

"That is exactly what I was thinking, Castorina," Perch agreed.

"Does he have a subscription to the Courier?"

"Yes, we know that he does. I went to the Kroger's near his house and picked up these freebie papers last week."

"We should also check Craigslist if we are looking for an ad for an old car that matches or is similar to the Honda."

"Have we checked KYDOT for any title transfers in the past three weeks, sometime after the ATM withdrawal narrows it down, but lets be conservative. And lets make it for any cars more than six years old. It's a wide net, but we have no choice."

"Perfh, we already know that the plate was from Indiana. That eliminates KYDOT. It could have been a hit and run by someone in town for a party, a wedding, the fair."

"Check Indiana as well, but coming on Sharon's previous 'accident', I don't see this being an unfortunate coincidence."

As Castor stood to leave, a sergeant entered, followed by a patrolman.

"Perch, Cas, this is patrolman Hardison. Tell them what you told me.

"This may be nothing, but the other day, I ticketed a car that meets your description. It was a charcoal grey, 1983 Honda civic, pretty beat up."

Percheron picked up one of the older weekly papers and began scanning the ads.

"With an Indiana tag?" Ertras said expectantly.

"No, Kentucky."

"Darn."

"Where did you ticket the vehicle patrolman Hardison?"

"Right here in downtown, on Chestnut, near a strip club. It was Two days ago."

"Do you have the tag number with you?"

"Yes, I have it right here."

Percheron folded the paper, circled one of the ads in blue ink, picked up his desk phone and placed a call.

"Good work Hardison. Hang on a minute."

"Hello, yes I am calling about the 83 Honda for sale. I see, you sold it a week ago or so? May I ask who you sold it to?".

There was a pause, then the detective spoke again in a more official voice.

"This is detective Henry Percheron from the Louisville Police Department. We are trying to trace that particular vehicle. Yes this is really the Louisville police. I can do that, but I was hoping that we could do this over the phone. Can you at least tell me license tag number? As much as you recall of it."

Perch repeated the digits for the benefit of Hardison. XAG were the last three digits?

Hardison looked at his sheet, smiled, looked at Perch and gave a thumbs up.

"Great, that matches. We can look up your address or, ok, great, that's fine. I should be there in about twenty minutes."

After he hung up, Perch asked the partrolman, "Good work, patrolman. What is your full name? I'll need it for our report."

"Joseph Wayne Hardison," the patrolman replied, his demeanor calm, but his heart racing.

Perch and Cas, along with the pleased patrolman, drove to an address in Shively, where they obtained confirmation that the car that had been ticketed had been the one sold, based on the general condition and the license plate. The seller also identified a photograph of Bruce Favor as being the man who bought the vehicle for $500.

"Did you transfer the title to this man?"

"I just took the money and gave him the keys. He said that he would handle the paperwork."

"Where were you on the night of August 3, around 9:30 pm?"

"Probably at Paddy's. I'm there just about every night."

"Did you drive there?"

"In what? I just told you that I sold my friggin' car. I went to Paddy's with a buddy."

"This is fine, Mr. Franks. You have been very helpful. We can check on the friend later, if we need to. We have enough for now," Percheron said, terminating the quetioning.

Their next stop was the strip club, hoping to have one of the dancers or employees place Favor there two nights ago, but no one identified Favor.

In response to numerous questions about who was in the club at the time, they met dead end after dead end. Like most nights, It was the same cast of no name patrons with the same face of half intoxicated desperation and anger.

Except for the booze, that description could fit Favor, but the dancers were unanimous in their statements that he had not been there.

The police trio left, disappointed.

"If not Favor, then was the person driving the car the killer?" Hardison queried from the rear seat.

Percheron responded aloud but spoke as if to himself.

"An accomplice? That's logical but why the different plate? That shouts deliberation and planning, while getting a ticket at a strip club was the opposite. Did Favor resell the car to a third person, just to recoup a couple of hundred dollars? That was stupid, and Favor is not stupid.

Plus, there was no recent cash deposit. Was the car payment for the killing? Possibly, but that was a loose end. It comes back to the plate change.

In my opinion, avarice and boredom combined in Favor to form an invisible, powerful explosive. And then, boom. I think that is the why of this murder. We all know the how and the when and the where. It comes down to the car. Cars are harder to dispose of than a gun, you can't just throw it in the river, or toss it into a dumpster.

"So Favor buys this car, we are sure of that," Ertras stated.

"Someone else later drives the car to commit the murder and then keeps it? . We are not sure of that," added Percheron.

"Who would Favor have given the car to?"

"Suppose that he did not know that he gave the car to someone?"

"He left it to be stolen? And have the blame for the hit and run assigned to the thief? That is clever."

"True, but why did he change the plate. Even with that change, once we find the car, we can trace it to him on the buy side. What are we missing?"

Ertras offered another question in lieu of an answer.

"Who would buy or steal such an old beater? It is not a collectible, it can't be all that reliable, it's ready

"To be scrapped. That is it. It all ties together. Let's go," Percheron exclaimed.

"Where?" queried Ertras

As way of answer, Perch turned to face the policeman in the rear seat.

"Patrolman Josesph Wayne Hardison, thanks to your tip, we've gotten a field trip to Shively, a jaunt to a strip club, and now we are off to the junkyard east of downtown. All of this in one day and you are not even yet officiallly on the homicide team. Let's go," he repeated.

When the two detectives and the uniformed policeman exited their vehicle in front on the office of the large, sprawling salvage yard, many of the outdoor workers walked quickly away. This was clearly going to end badly for someone.

The manager of the salvage yard, a Jim Murnaghan, was relieved to find that they were looking for information on a car, and not looking to arrest an employee. He did a quick search of his files and confirmed that they did in fact have that car. It was still in the yard.

"We leave the car set for a few days just in case the car is reported stolen or the owner has a change of heart."

"Does that happen often?"

"That the car is stolen? Sometimes, but we check when we buy the car. There can be a time lag, say the car is stolen from the airport while the owner is out of town, something like that."

"And the other? Where the owner changes their mind?"

"More than you would think."

"What do you do then?"

"We usually sell it back to them."

"Usually?"

"This is a business."

"So you sell it back to them at a profit."

"For more than you would think."

"What about this one?"

"We are just about to crush it."

"Don't. We need to look at it."

"No problem, detective. I can show it to you now.

As they walked from the office to the crushing area, Perch asked, "While these cars are in quarantine, waiting to be crushed, do you drive them?"

"Off the yard, you mean?"

"Yes."

"That's against policy, but it's been known to happen. The guys who work here may need a car once in a while."

"To do what?"

"What does a person do with a car?"

"Do your guys ever go to the strip club on Chestnut?"

"Are you serious? How would I know?" Murnaghan answered swiftly.

"I suppose that they do. Listen, I crush cars. I'm not a traffic cop and I'm not a chaperone for grown men. There it is," Murnaghan said, pointing at the vehicle."

A dozer had just flipped the vehicle onto its side.

"Tell your man to stop."

"Sure. OK." The manager waved the operator off.

"That was close, Perch, five minutes later and the car would have been flattened," Ertras exclaimed.

Murnaghan corrected her with a smile.

"You had more than five minutes, ma'am", not sure how to address a female detective.

"This is just the first step. We need to remove some parts."

"Which parts?"

"Well, the catalytic converter for one. It contains palladium. We burn them off and sell them on to a precious metals wholesaler. Here, I'll show you."

The quartet approached the car. Off to one side a short man with an acetylene torch stood by, bored by their presence.

Something caught Perch's eye, an object wedged up in the frame, a woman's small handbag. He gripped it and yanked several times before he was able to extract it from the niche in which it nestled, nearly slicing his hand in the process.

He opened the bag, extracted a wallet, and from it withdrew the driver's license of the late Sharon Favor.

Perch showed it to his colleagues, then addressed Murnaghan.

"Do you have the seller's name?"

"Yes, back in the office."

Once returned to the office, the yard manager retrieved the relevant file, and holding it in his hand, he stated, "We bought it from an Emile Jackson.

"Not a Bruce Favor?"

"No, who's he?"

"Do you have a transferred title?"

"No."

"Why not?"

"In Kentucky, if the vehicle is more than twelve years old, then no title is needed. Blame KYDOT, not me."

"Favor is clever, Perch."

"Yes he is."

"This was his plan, buy an old car that he could get rid of, no questions asked. If the Honda had been destroyed, there would be nothing to link a Kentucky tagged vehicle to the crime, and no reason for us to connect Favor and the seller.

Now we know from the seller that Favor bought the car. On the seller side, someone named Jackson sold it. Two men working together."

"I don't think so, Castorina. Mr. Murnaghan, do you recognize this man?" Perch was holding a photograph of Bruce Favor for the manager to see.

"Absolutely, that is Mr. Jackson."

"You must deal with a lot of people. How can you be so confident, that this is Emile Jackson?"

"When we buy a car we ask for ID. That is the face from Jackson's driver's license."

"Are you certain?"

"Of course. See for yourself," handing over the dossier. "We make a xerox copy of the driver's license for our files."

"Is that legal?" Hardison queried.

"Inside my yard it is."

"Does the seller know that you make a copy?"

"You'd have to ask them." Murnaghan paused, then added, "Probably not."

Percheron smiled, "He will soon."

Perch was quiet on the short ride back to the police station.

It's possible that Bruce Favor may have never acted on his cravings if Perch's arrival was not perceived as an I dare you, an invitation to play against a talented adversary.

Perch did not believe this was the case, his experience told him that the fuse was already burning. He had failed to extinguish it, but the detective was neither the igniter nor an accelerant.

He had hoped that a preventative dose of policing reality on the stormy mind of a would be criminal would end the affair before it began. It had been a risk worth taking. If he believed otherwise, we would be forever frozen in inaction, himself a victim. He would be useless in his vocation. Nevertheless, he understood that once again his role had been that of a pathologist and not that of a healer.

TWELVE

"Hello. Sharon?"

"What?"

"I'm sorry. I was startled."

"So am I."

"I thought for a moment that you were Sharon, but you can't be"

"I'm Vicky, Sharon's older sister."

"Yes, I can see that. I have this old photograph. I can see the resemblance. And the difference. I'm rude. I only meant"

"I remember that photo, I gave it to a man named Percheron. He was a police detective. But that was years ago. You aren't he, are you?"

"No, he died, about a year ago. You hadn't heard."

"No. I remember him as a kind man. I've been living overseas for a few years now. I only recently returned to the States."

After my initial surprise, it was evident that Vicky was not Sharon. She was a sister, but that entailed being her own person. I had leapt hastily to the least likely conclusion – a ghost. . I plead that I was weak, not physically but mentally fatigued. I had never smelled myself both so alive and so near death, the phrase is contradictory but it is even now, after the fact, the best that I can conjure.

It was the facial structure of the two women, it was familial and due certainly to some unknown origin, more residue of this strange affair, familiar to me.

And there there was the color, the dress. Vicky's robe was yellow, but a much better quality, very fashionable today as far as I understand fashion.

My sister liked yellow, it was her best and favorite color.

"I flew back from Asia upon hearing the news. It was difficult, don't ask how I managed the flight during this pandemic. I would have sailed my boat over but it's strange, I've come to appreciate crowds, despite this damned virus."

"I'm sorry if I am interrupting. I did not expect anyone to be here."

"Were you a friend of Bruce?"

"No, I never met him."

"If you had, you would have certainly not have wanted him as friend."

"No, I guess not."

"They preach not to speak ill of the dead, but I say, why change now? He was a horrible person. He died too late. Enough about him. Did you know Sharon?"

"Yes. No. I mean I think so."

"You've covered all the available responses. Should I ask you something simpler?"

" I, I'm sorry. You won't believe me, I'm not sure that I believe it, or myself, myself. I sound crazy, but I don't think that I am."

"Visiting the long dead in this manicured mausoleum is crazy. Yet we do it, repeatedly.

You claim that I won't believe you, but a cemetery is the perfect place to believe. Tell me."

I recounted the two sightings of her sister, one just yesterday, her clothes and odd appearance, her photo in Percheron's book of the dead. I described Martin Aiken's theory, without disclosing his name.

I came here to.. Frankly I have no idea."

"I am having Sharon exhumed in a few days and moved. I'm not sure why I feel compelled to tell you. I needed to tell someone who cared, and you may fit the bill."

I remained silent, as once again I did not know the correct answer.

It must have been a suitable response, for she continued.

"If it is truly to death us do part, why bury a deceased widow next to her late husband. Doesn't she have an out clause, one based on time served?"

I heard a mockingbird call from a nearby tree. I said nothing.

"This is worse", she exclaimed, indicating the shared tombstone before us. "Freshly engraved with grooves of deceit."

She took a breath, held it, exhaled, took another breath and rebegan speaking.

"I wasn't always wealthy. If I had been, if I had been, we always find excuses, don't we?"

I said nothing. What is there to say to truth?

She looked at me curiously.

"You say nothing. That's fine. I need to speak, not to listen. It's just that your presence here is like some phantom, one who haunts under the full sun. I guess we are both crazy. I comfort and berate myself with 'If I had been.' If I had been wealthy, life and death would have different.

I wanted to move her years ago, when Bruce was first arrested. That was after her burial, of course. And he was still her husband. He had appeal after appeal, delay followed delay. He won. Justice is never served. There must be a reason why courthouses are carved with false words from a dead language."

Bruce died of a stroke just recently. That is why I flew back. Not to attend his funeral," she added in response to my surprised look.

"His next of kin, decided to bury his distant cousin here, next to Sharon. The grave was already paid for, it's a pity that had he known, he could have sold this site, thrown Bruce into a less expensive plot somewhere else, and pocketed the difference. He'd have made out well, this plot was all that Bruce had of value. He lost all that was valuable when he elected to purchase a 13 year old car.

You can reside next door to someone for years and not really know them. Living with someone may result in the same ignorance."

I was puzzled as to what that meant, but I kept my face expressionless.

"Sharon is dead. But now he is dead as well. And I will write my own words, for myself and for Sharon."

I did not ask Vicky where Sharon would be reinterred. If Bruce were listening, I did not want him to hear.

As I finish this book, I ask myself what I should do with Percheron's photo album. Should I keep it, turn it over to some police museum, or donate it to Frazier's, which combined, local, international and eclectic exhibits? Or should I destroy it? I will think on it a while longer.

Vicky said she was going to move her sister to a safe place. If she had been my sister and if I had the resources of Vicky I know of only one place for her to rest in peace.

EDITOR'S POSTSCRIPT

I regret to inform the reader that as this unsettling story was going to print, I learned that its author had died, a victim of COVID-19.

As part of the estate settlement, the author's home in Lake Forest was put up for sale and a local real estate company was tasked with the preparation and subsequent sale of the property.

During the open house, the home was so immaculate that neighbors and prospective buyers who attended asked for the contact information of the cleaning service.

This proved to be a fruitless quest, as no one at the real estate office recalled ever engaging a service.

One of the residents on the same street, a Kylie Button, remembered seeing a 30ish or so blonde woman departing the house, carrying a large number of bags, cleaning materials, Ms. Button assumed.

As editor, I requested that the realtor retain the so-called Book of the Dead for our publication staff to review. This book was never located.

FIN